Please return or renew this item before the latest date shown below

CUPAR
LIBRARY
1 3 NOV 2019

1 7 DEC 2019

−1 FEB 2020

4 APR 2020

1 7 DEC 2020

1 4 JUN 2022

1 6 SEP 2022

2 7 APR 2023

2 6 AUG 2023

2 8 NOV 2023

Renewals can be made
by internet   www.onfife.com/fife-libraries
in person   at any library in Fife
by phone   03451 55 00 66

ON
AT FIFE
LIBRARIES

Thank you for using your library

The Five Mile Press
1 Centre Road, Scoresby
Victoria 3179 Australia
www.fivemile.com.au

ISBN 978 1 74300 328 2

Printed in China 5 4 3 2 1

Schooltime
for Sammy

The Five Mile Press

While his brother and sister got ready for the first day of school, Sammy climbed his favourite tree and swung from branch to branch.

Fred called up, 'You're old enough to go to school this year, Sammy.'

'I don't want to go to school! I want to stay home and play!' replied Sammy.

'But school is fun, and you'll learn all
kinds of things,' said Sophie.
'I'm not going!' said Sammy,
dangling upside-down and pulling a face.
'I already know everything. I know how to climb
the tallest trees and I can swing really fast. So there!'
Fred and Sophie rushed off to school.

Sammy spent the morning playing but soon got bored.
'What's wrong, Sammy?' asked his mother.
'There's nobody to play with,' said Sammy grumpily.
'Well, all your friends are at school,' explained
his mother. 'Maybe you should go, too.'
'No way!' shouted Sammy,
scrambling back up the tree.

At last, Sophie and Fred returned home,
chattering excitedly about their busy day.
Sammy ran to greet them.

Sammy wanted Fred and Sophie to play with him,
but they said that they had homework to do.
Sammy did not want to be left out.
'I can do homework too,' he said.
'How many days are there in April?' Fred asked Sophie.
'Twenty-five ninety zillion!' shouted Sammy.
'Oh, Sammy, don't be silly. We're trying to work,'
said Sophie with a sigh.

When Sammy's friend Jack came to visit,
he was full of news about school.
'The teacher is really nice, and I've learned lots of
important things,' said Jack proudly. 'I know what
two plus one plus two is.'
'So do I!' said Sammy, trying to count on his fingers.
'What is it then?' asked Jack.
'It's, um, it's … a lot!' Sammy answered.

'I even learned how to write my own name,'
Jack continued. He picked up a stick and carefully
wrote J-A-C-K in the dirt.

'I can write my name too. Look!' said Sammy.
'That's just a scribble,' scoffed Jack.
Poor Sammy felt embarrassed.

'What else did you do at school?' asked Sammy.
'Well, I made lots of new friends and we
all played games together,' said Jack.

Then Jack told Sammy everything
that he had learned. His favourite part of the day
was Show and Tell, when people could bring in
special things and share them with the class.
'You really did do a lot,' said Sammy with a sad sigh.

'I'll paint you a picture of a tree, if you want,'
offered Jack, to cheer up his friend.
'That's another thing I learned today!'
Sammy watched as Jack brushed paint over a piece of paper.
'That's the best picture in the whole world!'
said Sammy admiringly.

When Jack had gone, Sammy tried to draw
a tree himself, but his painting just
looked like a messy blob.

That night at dinner, Sammy was very quiet.
He did not feel like eating anything.
Sophie and Fred chattered loudly about school.
'I got a gold star on my spelling test,' bragged Sophie.
'I won a race at playtime,' said Fred proudly.
'Well done, both of you,' said their parents.

After dinner, Sammy decided that he wanted
to be as clever as his brother and sister.
He crept quietly over to Sophie's
school bag and slipped out a book.
He sat in a corner and tried to read it.
But the words just looked like squiggles.

When Sophie and Fred found Sammy
with the book, they read him the story.
It was a thrilling tale about pirates.

The next morning, Sammy woke up very early.
He found his school bag and packed Effalump,
his favourite toy, carefully inside.
He wanted to have something for Show and Tell.
Sammy marched into the kitchen
and announced, 'I'm ready!'

Sammy's family looked up in surprise.
'Ready for what, Sammy?' asked his father.
'I am going to school,' declared Sammy.
'I want to learn how to read and write
and count and draw beautiful pictures.'
'That's wonderful,' said his mother.

After breakfast, Sammy set off with Sophie
and Fred. He made them walk very quickly.
'I'm already a day late for school,' he said.
'I don't want to miss any more!'